GO THERE, MAMA BEAR

written by
Shawna Danberg

illustrated by
Jennifer Davison

Text © Shawna Danberg 2023

Illustrations © Jennifer Davison 2023

All rights reserved.

No part of this book may be reproduced, stored in a retrieval system, or transmitted in any form or by any means, electronic, mechanical, photocopy, recording or otherwise, without written permission of the publisher.

Paperback ISBN: 978-1-955546-52-2

Hardcover ISBN: 978-1-955546-51-5

Dedication

To the mama bears around
the world standing for truth,

and to Kenzie and Tyra,
the fierce mama bears
of my grand baby bears.

I love you.

A mama bear loves,
a mama bear cares,

a mama bear protects her little baby bears.

A mama bear holds,
a mama bear squeezes,

a mama bear finds tissues
when her baby bear sneezes.

A mama bear leads,
a mama bear preaches,

a mama bear instructs baby bear on what the Bible teaches.

A mama bear hugs,
a mama bear kisses,

a mama bear corrects when baby bear misses.

A mama bear fasts,
a mama bear prays,

a mama bear worships as baby bear plays.

A mama bear multiplies,
a mama bear trains,

a mama bear knows baby bear
will soon lead the way.

A mama bear encourages, a mama bear beams,

a mama bear listens
to all of baby bear's dreams.

A mama bear discerns, a mama bear is strong,

a mama bear shows baby bear what is right from wrong.

A mama bear stands,
a mama bear unites,

a mama bear helps baby bear understand our rights.

A mama bear uses her voice,
a mama bear declares,

"Go there, Mama Bear!" to anyone who hears.

A mama bear loves,
a mama bear cares,

a mama bear protects her little baby bears.

Mama Bear Declaration

I will pray.
TODAY, I will lift up my children to the Lord.
No weapon formed against me
or my family will prosper.
Since God is for me, who can be against me?
Therefore, I will mother from a place of rest,
knowing the King of the universe is in control.

I will fast.
TODAY, I will fight for my children,
waging war in worship and intercession.
I will protect my children at all costs.
Therefore, I give up temporary comforts
now to preserve our freedom and our future.

I will stand.
TODAY, I won't back down from the truth.
I am strong, courageous, and ready.
I will battle in the spiritual and the natural realm.
Therefore, I will use my voice and
take my space wherever I am called to "GO."

I will multiply.
TODAY, I will instruct my children in the Lord,
discerning the influences in their lives at every turn.
Boldly I will lead, guide, and show them the way.
Therefore, I will encourage them to step out in faith,
remembering I was made for this and so were they.

Baby Bear Declaration

I am brave.
I am strong.
I was made for this.

I will learn.
I will pray.
I was made for this.

I will lead.
I will stand.
I was made for this.

God is with me.
God is for me.
I was made for this!

Acknowledgments

Eastyn, Charlie, Paisley, Stevie,
and Hudson, you inspired me to write
this book. May you always live wild
and free for Jesus.

To our sons Preston and Riley,
I honor the way you care for,
provide for, and protect your families.
You are fantastic daddy bears.

To David Sluka, thank you for your edits,
education, and encouragement.

And to the best papa bear of them all,
my legendary husband, JD. This book
wouldn't have happened without
your yes. Thank you for
supporting me always.

Shawna Danberg is an author, speaker, and life coach. She is a mother and grandmother who married her high school sweetheart. Her passion is helping others live a life of wholeness, freedom, and complete victory in Jesus.

You can learn more about Shawna and her work at www.victorymindsetcoaching.com
@shawna_danberg

Jennifer Davison is a renowned illustrator who has illustrated over fifty picture books. She spends most of her time illustrating faith-based books and stories from the Bible, including the Very Best Bible Stories series and *God's Big Promises Bible Storybook*.

You can learn more about Jennifer and her work at www.jensketches.com
@jen_sketch

Printed in the USA
CPSIA information can be obtained
at www.ICGtesting.com
LVRC080926181223
766705LV00043B/116